First published by Parragon in 2013
Parragon
Chartist House
15–17 Trim Street
Bath BA1 1HA, UK
www.parragon.com

ISBN 978-1-78186-579-8

Printed in China

Disney · PIXAR
MONSTERS
UNIVERSITY

MU
SCARERS
MU
MONSTERS

Parragon
Bath • New York • Singapore • Hong Kong • Cologne • Delhi
Melbourne • Amsterdam • Johannesburg • Shenzhen

When Mike Wazowski was six years old, he went on a trip with his class. Mike was the smallest monster at Frighton Elementary, and the least popular.

Nobody wanted to be Mike's partner, so Mrs Graves took Mike's hand. Mike gave her a weak smile. Then he began pulling her towards Monsters, Inc.

Inside Monsters, Inc., Mike snuck away from Mrs Graves. Although he knew that human children were deadly to monsters, he crossed the red safety line. He followed one of the Scarers through a door into the human world.

Mike watched as the Scarer frightened a sleeping child. It was the most amazing thing Mike had ever seen! He decided that he wanted to be a Scarer when he grew up.

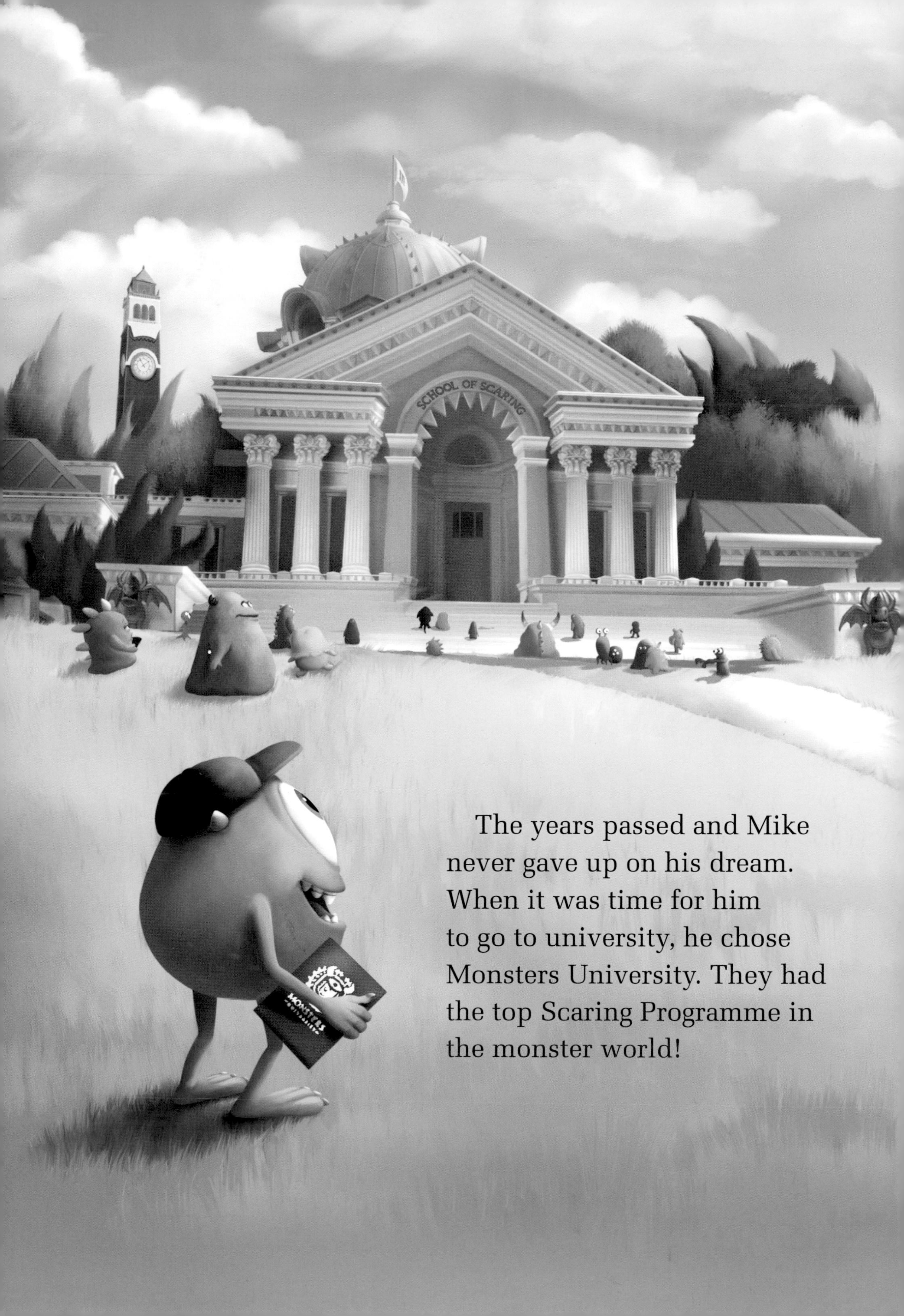

The years passed and Mike never gave up on his dream. When it was time for him to go to university, he chose Monsters University. They had the top Scaring Programme in the monster world!

But Monsters University wasn't just about studying. There were all kinds of clubs to join, too.

The President and Vice President of the Greek Council handed Mike a leaflet. "We sponsor the annual Scare Games," they said.

"It's a super-intense scaring competition!" said the VP. "You get a chance to prove you're the best."

Mike thought that the Scare Games sounded amazing!

Mike's roommate was a friendly monster named Randy Boggs. He amazed Mike by disappearing – and reappearing – without warning.

Mike thought Randy's talent was awesome. "But lose the glasses," he told him. "They give it away."

On the first day of classes, Mike and Randy went to a class in the School of Scaring building. Suddenly, head of the Scaring Programme, Dean Hardscrabble, swooped in. Hardscrabble was terrifying. When she was a professional Scarer, she broke the all-time scare record.

"At the end of the semester, there will be a final exam," said Hardscrabble. "Fail that exam and you are out of the Scaring Programme."

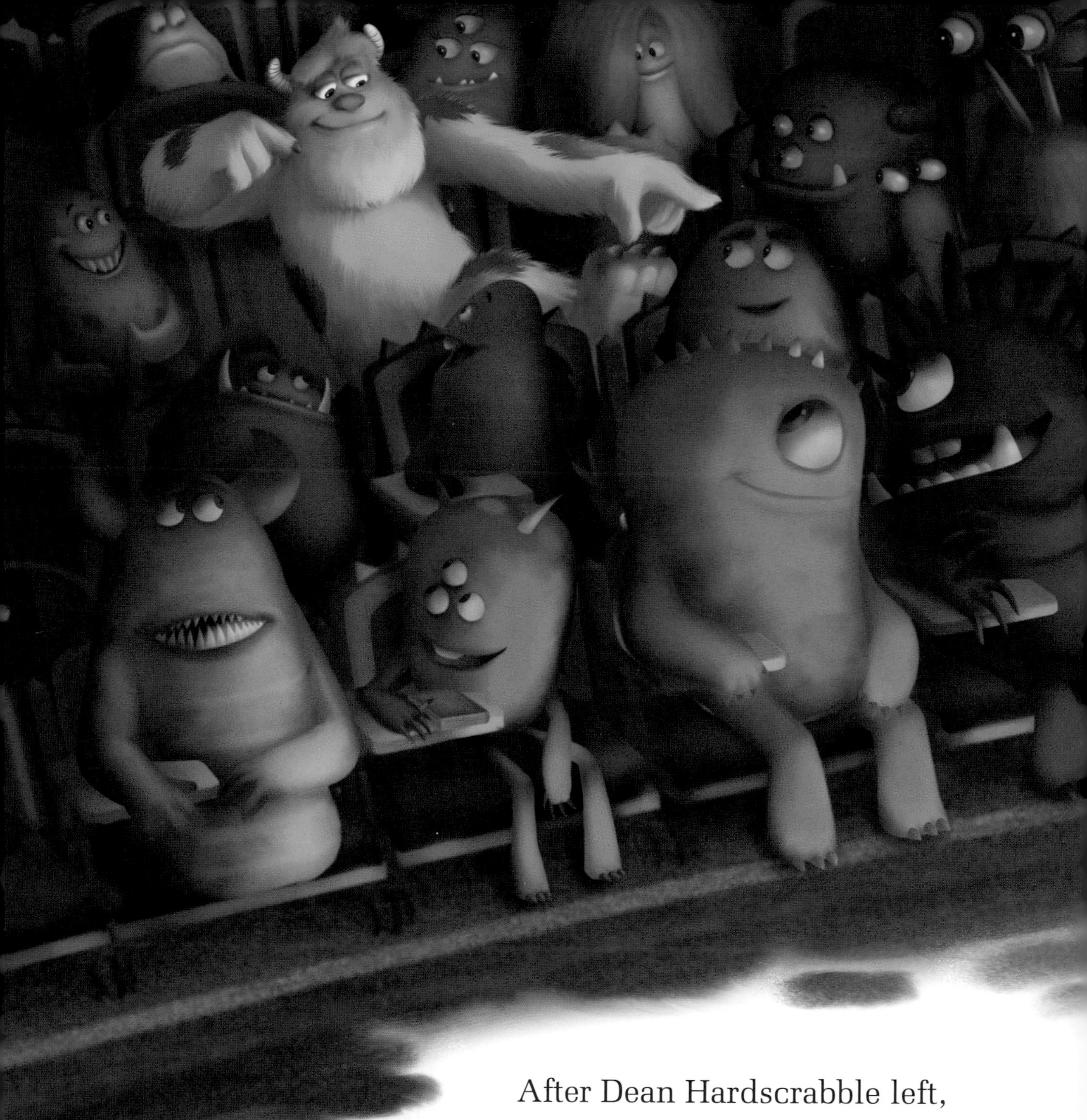

After Dean Hardscrabble left, Professor Knight asked, "Who can tell me the properties of an effective roar?"

Mike's hand shot up. He was giving his answer when an enormous "ROAR!" came from the back of the classroom. It was James P. Sullivan, or Sulley for short. He was a huge blue monster and the son of a famous Scarer, Bill Sullivan.

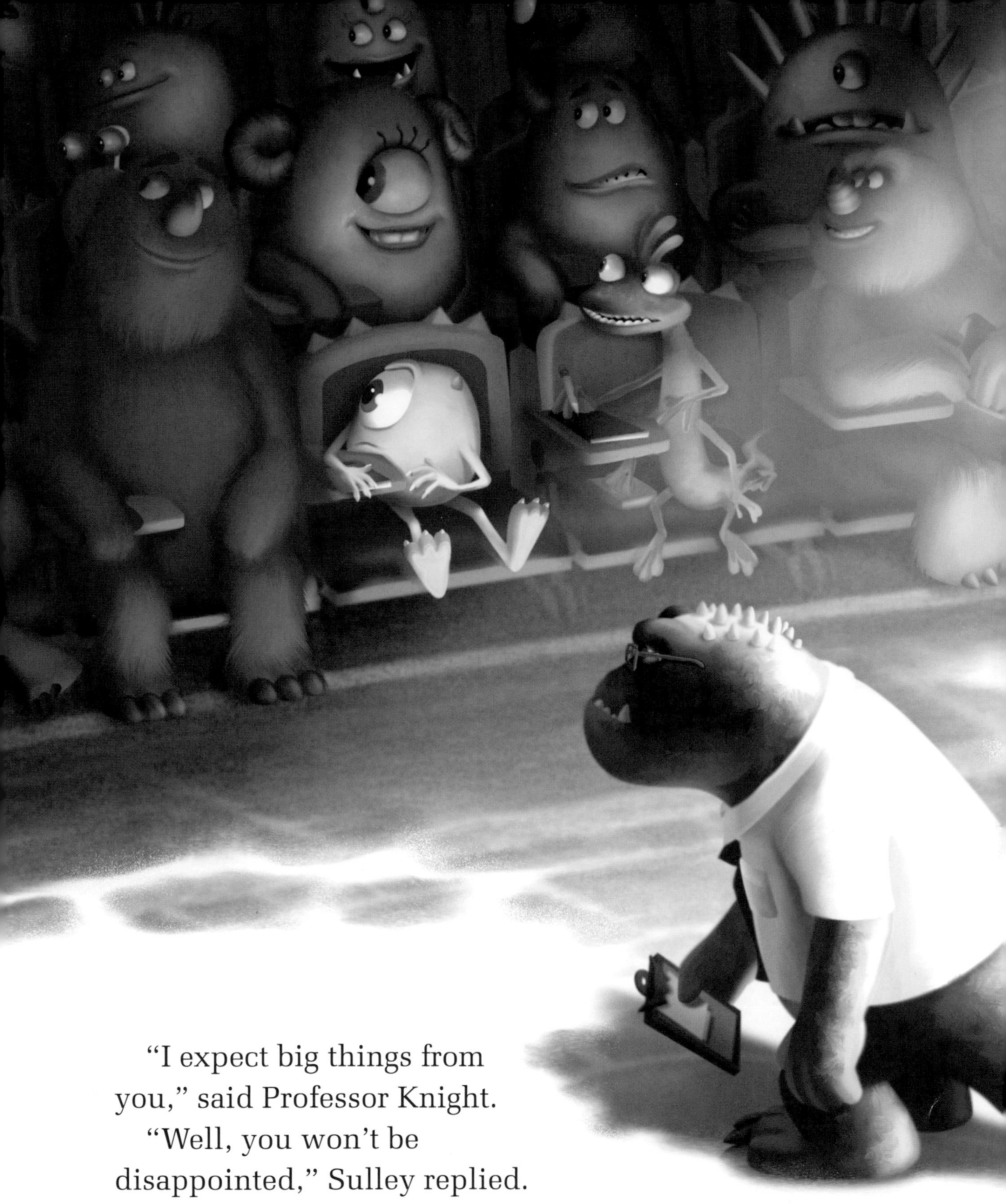

“I expect big things from you,” said Professor Knight.

“Well, you won’t be disappointed,” Sulley replied.

Mike was annoyed. Sulley had come to class late, ruined his answer and hadn’t even brought a pencil and notebook!

After the class, Mike went back to his room to study. He was going to spend every waking moment getting ready for the scaring final.

Then suddenly, an animal came flying through Mike's window – followed by Sulley! Sulley had stolen the mascot of rival school, Fear Tech.

Archie the Scare Pig grabbed Mike's MU hat and leapt back out of the window.

Mike ran after Archie and hopped onto his back to try and stop him. But the Scare Pig kept running, and Sulley wasn't far behind! The three went on a wild chase through a party.

Finally, Mike trapped Archie in a rubbish bin. Sulley scooped up both Mike and Archie and held them proudly above his head.

Now everyone thought Sulley had captured Archie. Roar Omega Roar, the top club on campus, was impressed!

Johnny, the president of ROR, invited Sulley to a party. When Mike tried to follow them, Sulley turned him away. “This is a party for scare students who actually have a chance,” said Sulley.

“My chances are as good as yours!” Mike shot back angrily. He promised Sulley he would scare circles around him in the coming year.

Mike worked harder than anybody in the Scaring Programme. He read every book he could find on scaring. He practised making frightening faces in the mirror. He asked Randy to test him day and night. Before long, Mike was acing all of his exams!

Sulley, meanwhile, was messing around and having fun. His grades showed it. Johnny gave Sulley a warning – if he didn't get better grades, he'd be kicked out of ROR.

On the day of the scare final, Mike and Sulley started to argue about who was scariest. Before long, they were roaring at each other.

Everyone began to notice Mike and Sulley – including Dean Hardscrabble. She was looking right at Sulley when he stumbled back and knocked her record-breaking scream can to the floor!

"I am so sorry!" cried Mike.

"It was an accident!" insisted Sulley.

Dean Hardscrabble stayed strangely calm. Then, after thinking about it, she decided neither Mike or Sulley would be staying in the Scaring Programme! They couldn't believe it.

The next term, Mike and Sulley were put in the Scream Can Design Programme. They found the classes very boring. Sulley blamed Mike for getting him kicked out of the Scaring Programme and ROR.

But one day, Mike found the Scare Games leaflet he'd picked up on his first day. He suddenly smiled. The Scare Games were the answer to all of his problems! Mike grabbed the leaflet and ran out of the door.

The Scare Games sign-ups were just finishing. Mike proposed a deal to Dean Hardscrabble: if his team won, she would have to let them all into the Scaring Programme.

Dean Hardscrabble agreed – but if they lost, Mike would have to leave Monsters University for good.

Mike needed to join a club to take part in the games. Only the Oozma Kappas would have him. But they still needed one more member....

"The star player has just arrived," said Sulley.

Mike was furious, but he had no choice – without Sulley they wouldn't be allowed to compete.

A little while later, Mike and Sulley arrived at their new house. The other OKs – Don, Squishy, Terri and Terry and Art – greeted them enthusiastically.

Mike and Sulley soon discovered that not one of the OKs was in the Scaring Programme.

"I'm gonna carry the whole team," Mike told Sulley.

"Really?" asked Sulley. "Who's gonna carry you?"

That night, Mike and Sulley met Ms Squibbles doing the laundry in the basement ... the Oozma Kappas lived in Squishy's mum's house!

Soon it was time for the first Scare Games event, the Toxicity Challenge. The teams had to get through a pitch black sewer tunnel filled with stinging glow urchins, as quickly as possible.

Mike and Sulley ran ahead and left the other OKs behind. The Roar Omega Roars finished first. Mike and Sulley crossed the line second, but because the rest of their team came in last, the OKs were out.

But then another team was disqualified for cheating. The OKs were back in!

The next day Mike gathered the OKs for a team meeting. They wanted to show Mike their 'talents'.

Don said he was stealthy, but his tentacles made noise every time he lifted them off the ground. Then Terri and Terry claimed they were masters of close-up magic, but their card trick didn't work.

Sulley wanted to ditch the OKs and find another team. But the game rules didn't allow it. Mike said that they had to do things his way from now on.

Sulley walked away. He thought that the OKs were hopeless.

The next event in the Scare Games was Avoid the Parent. The teams had to make their way through the library and capture a flag without getting caught by the librarian. If they got caught, the librarian would grab them with her giant tentacles and launch them out of the library.

Mike told everyone to move slowly and quietly. But Sulley got impatient and climbed a book ladder. He zipped sideways towards the flag.

Then, suddenly, there was a loud CRACK! The ladder broke and Sulley crashed to the floor!

The librarian turned to Sulley, but Don distracted her by making noises with his tentacles. Then Terri and Terry created a distraction to save Don – and Art created a distraction to save Terri and Terry. Mike didn't know what was going on!

The librarian gave chase. Finally, the OKs made it out of the back door of the library.

"Woo-hoo! We did it!" yelled Art.

"No, we didn't. We forgot the flag!" said Mike.

Just then, Squishy surprised them all by appearing with the flag! The OKs took fourth place!

Nearby, an unhappy Hardscrabble looked on. She couldn't believe the OKs were still in the Scare Games.

That night, the OKs were invited to a party at the ROR house. They were thrilled!

Everyone at the party gave the Oozma Kappas a warm welcome. It felt strange – their classmates weren't usually this nice to them. The OKs relaxed and began to have fun. They even busted out their best dance moves!

Then Johnny introduced the OKs. “The surprise team of the Scare Games!” he said. “Oozma Kappa!”

Suddenly paint showered down on them, and the entire room burst into laughter. It was all a set-up!

The next day, photos of the Oozma Kappas covered in paint were everywhere.

“Real Scarers look like us, not like you,” Johnny told Mike.

The OKs were feeling down in the dumps. But luckily, Mike had an idea. “Guys, I’ve been doing this all wrong. We’re going on a field trip,” he announced.

Ms Squibbles drove them to Monsters, Inc., where Mike broke open the gate. Then he led the others onto the roof. It had a perfect view of a scare floor.

“Take a good look, fellas,” said Mike. “See what they all have in common?”

"No, not really," Squishy replied.

"Exactly," said Mike. "The best Scarers use their differences to their advantage."

While all the OKs watched the action on the scare floor, Mike and Sulley both admitted that they had behaved badly. They agreed that they needed to start working together as a team.

The next morning, Mike and Sulley woke up bright and early and leapt out of bed. They packed up their gear and put on the OK uniforms that Ms Squibbles had sewn for them.

Then they headed off to Scare Games practice!

Mike trained the OKs in everything they would need to know for the next two events. He taught them how to scare kids and avoid parents and teenagers. He taught them how to hide. He even got them to run on the spot with 'scary feet' to make sure they were in tip-top shape.

By the time of the fourth event, Hide and Sneak, there were only three teams left: ROR, HSS and OK. All the competitors had to hide in a dark house while several referees roamed the rooms searching for them with torches.

The HSS team were soon discovered – but no one else was found.

That meant the RORs and the OKs would compete against each other for the Scare Games trophy! The RORs couldn't figure out how the Oozma Kappas had come so far.

Later that day, Sulley spoke to Dean Hardscrabble.

"When we get back into the Scaring Programme, I hope there's no hard feelings," he said.

Dean Hardscrabble said she didn't think that they would win. Mike just wasn't scary enough. Sulley stood up for Mike, but he began to wonder if Hardscrabble was right....

That night, Sulley told Mike that he needed to stop *thinking* 'scary' and start *feeling* it. Mike tried to roar loudly, but Sulley wanted more.

"Let the animal out!" coached Sulley. "Dig deep!"

Mike gave it all he had. Sulley just hoped it would be enough to win.

The next day, the OKs got huge cheers from the crowd at the final event – everyone was rooting for them.

Each team member had to prove their skill by scaring a simulated child. The competition was neck and neck. The last two team members to compete were Mike and Johnny. "Don't take the loss too hard," Johnny sneered at Mike. "You never belonged here anyway."

Mike ignored him. He couldn't let anything distract him from doing his best.

Johnny entered his scare simulator and got a huge scream from his robot. He was certain he had won it for the RORs.

Next Mike entered his room. He closed his eyes. This was it. He took a deep breath and let out his most explosive roar! The robot child sat bolt upright and filled the scream can all the way to the top....

The OKs had won the Scare Games! The stadium cheered wildly as Mike walked out of the simulator.

The Roar Omega Roars were shocked. They never thought that they would lose the Scare Games – especially to the Oozma Kappas!

The OKs lifted Mike up into the air.

"We're in the Scaring Programme!" shouted Sulley.

OK
OK
OK

But then, Mike noticed his settings on the simulator. They had been changed from 'hard' to 'easy'. Sulley admitted that he had done it.

Mike was hurt and angry. "You said you believed in me, but you're just like everyone else!" he yelled and stormed away.

The other Oozma Kappas heard everything. They were heartbroken. Sulley felt awful.

Mike stormed off angrily and headed straight to the Door Tech department. He swiped a key to the lab where students tested doors to the human world. He was going to prove to everyone once and for all that he was scary!

Mike quietly entered a room in the human world through a wardrobe door. He rolled across the floor and ruffled the curtains. Next, he crept closer to the child's bed.

Mike leapt up. "ROAR!" he cried as scarily as he could.

The child just looked at Mike and smiled. "You look funny," she said.

Mike couldn't believe it. His Scare hadn't worked! Then he suddenly realized that he wasn't in a child's bedroom. He was in a big room ...

... and it was full of kids! They were all looking at him. Mike had walked into a cabin full of campers!

Back in the Door Tech Lab, Hardscrabble and her guards were holding back a crowd. Mike had set the alarm off.

"No one goes through that door until the authorities arrive," she announced.

When Sulley arrived at the lab, the OKs were already there. Don turned to Sulley. "You don't think that could be –"

"It's Mike," Sulley said. He had worked out what his friend was doing.

"But he could die out there!" cried Squishy.

Sulley wasn't going to let that happen. While the other OKs distracted Hardscrabble, he slipped through the door into the human world.

Sulley was surprised to find an empty cabin. Where had Mike gone? Sulley went to the window and saw a group of adults outside.

Realizing that Mike had fled into the nearby forest, Sulley made a break from the cabin. The adults shone their torches on him as he disappeared into the trees.

"Bear!" they shouted.

Sulley found Mike sitting by a lake.

"You were right, they weren't scared of me," said Mike. "I thought I could show everybody that Mike Wazowski is something special … but I'm just not."

Sulley told Mike he wasn't much different. He had always messed things up, his entire life.

"I'll never know how you feel, but you're not the only 'failure' here," he said.

Just then the adults arrived. The pair ran back to the cabin. But when they opened the wardrobe – it was just a wardrobe. The door no longer led back to the monster world!

Sulley was worried. He could hear the adults getting closer to the cabin.

But Mike had an idea. "If we really scare them," he said, "we could generate enough screams to power the door from this side. Just follow my lead."

As the adults entered the cabin, Mike and Sulley turned on a fan, shook the shutters and fluttered the curtains. Then Mike slammed the door shut. Next came claw marks on the walls, followed by the bunk beds toppling over like dominoes!

The adults were terrified. “Aaaaahhhhh!” they screamed.

Suddenly, the wardrobe door started to light up!

Mike and Sulley regrouped up in the rafters. Their scare set-up had worked!

Mike looked at Sulley. "Are you ready?" he asked.

"Mike, I can't," Sulley replied.

"Yes, you can. Stop being a Sullivan and start being you!"

Mike jumped down from the rafters and gave Sulley the signal. The big blue monster made himself look even bigger. The adults stared at Sulley with shock and fear as he let out a deafening roar. The adults screamed ... and screamed ... and screamed!

In the Door Tech Lab, the light above the door glowed bright red. Its scream can filled to the brim. All the other scream cans in the room filled up, too!

Hardscrabble shielded her eyes from the blinding light. "Impossible!" she said.

Seconds later, Mike and Sulley burst through the door.

"How did you do this?" asked Hardscrabble in disbelief.

Just then, some Child Detection Agency agents burst into the wreckage of the lab. They grabbed Mike and Sulley and led them away.

Later, Sulley and Mike told the OKs that they had been expelled. The OKs had some news, too – Hardscrabble had let them into the Scaring Programme!

"You're the scariest bunch of monsters I ever met," said Mike. "Don't let anyone tell you different."

Everyone hugged goodbye. Then Mike and Sulley were on their way.

"So what now?" Sulley asked Mike.

Mike thought for a moment. "For the first time in my life, I don't really have a plan," he said.

A bus pulled up, and Mike and Sulley shook hands. Mike got on the bus, took a seat and stared out of the window.

Then suddenly, Mike heard a THUD! Sulley had grabbed onto the bus! The bus driver stopped and Mike got back off.

Sulley looked his friend in the eye. There was something he needed to tell him. "I don't know a single Scarer who can do what you do," said Sulley. "You're not scary, but you are fearless."

Just then Hardscrabble appeared with a copy of the school newspaper. Mike and Sulley were on the front page.

"You surprised me," admitted Hardscrabble. It was clear she admired their epic scare.

Mike looked at the newspaper. He saw the ad for mailroom workers at Monsters, Inc. that Johnny had shown him days earlier. Suddenly Mike had a new plan!

The friends got jobs working in the mailroom at Monsters, Inc.

They were starting at the bottom, but they didn't care. They knew that with hard work, there was nothing Team Wazowski and Sullivan couldn't do.

Mike and Sulley were the best workers Monsters, Inc. had ever seen. They quickly moved up the ranks of the company. It wasn't long before Mike and Sulley became Monsters, Inc.'s first scare team!

As Mike walked towards the scare floor, everyone wished him luck on his first day.

"You coming, coach?" called Sulley.

"You better believe it!" Mike replied. He stepped over the red safety line with a huge grin on his face. He was finally where he had always known he belonged!